T0196366

Bringing Down a

BULLY

Book Four

D.C. Marek

authorHOUSE®

AuthorHouse™ LLC
1663 Liberty Drive
Bloomington, IN 47403
www.authorhouse.com
Phone: 1-800-839-8640

Published by AuthorHouse 05/16/2014

ISBN: 978-1-4918-2425-2 (sc)
ISBN: 978-1-4918-2424-5 (e)

Library of Congress Control Number: 2013918001

In Loving Memory of Fletcher M. Krider-Koll
July 12 2012-April 12 2013

"An Angel in the Book of Life
wrote down this baby's birth,
and whispered as she closed the
Book . . . too beautiful for Earth."

To: The Koll Family:
PJ and Daughter, "Pip" McKenna

Also to a special friend, Anne Crawshaw:
She travels the Red Road with
Cotton and Maggie. (RIP Phoebe)

"I can do all things in Him who Strengthens me."

Philippians 4:13

FOREWORD

Fletcher was dressed for his first day of school at Stockton Elementary. He stood 4 feet, three inches tall and weighed 77 pounds; average for an eleven-year-old.

But, what wasn't average was his flaming red hair, brilliant blue eyes . . . . and the hump on his back. He tried to hide it as best he could, but the hump was still noticeable. Remarkably, that was okay with him.

The name Fletcher is Scottish for 'maker of arrows'. He liked that; yes indeed he did . . . .

CHAPTER ONE

Mike Decker and Jimmy Pittenger were neighbors and best friends since Jimmy moved to Stockton, Connecticut from Indiana. They were twelve-years-old and in the same 6th grade class at Stockton Elementary. Mike was heavier than Jimmy. He had brown hair, and was more impulsive compared to Jimmy who was thin, had blonde hair (which he was proud of as he regarded it passed down from his Viking ancestors), and was more the thinker of the two partly because of all the books he read. The stories of Sherlock Holmes were his favorite fiction books, while history, especially about the Presidents, was his favorite non-fiction. Mike's favorite reading material was comic books.

It was after lunch recess, which can be either fun or aggravating. It happened to be the latter as the two boys watched the school bully, Sam Newman, corner his newest victim.

"That Sam makes me so mad. He's such a loser," said Mike. "Let's go over there and stop him. Bullies like him are basically cowards when stood up to."

"Who's the kid he's picking on? First time I've seen him." said Jimmy.

"I don't know his name, but I know he's in fifth grade."

"How do you know what grade he's in?"

"I saw him with Mr. Burtt's class on their way to the lunch room."

"Well, since he's a new student, I think we should go over and make him feel welcomed . . . good excuse to get him away from Sam."

Mike and Jim were laughing as they approached Sam and two of his friends; if you could call them friends. Jason Brown and Ricky Hayes didn't fit in with most of the kids in school because of shyness and low self-esteem. Sam realized all this and took advantage by taking them on as sidekicks because they would do anything he asked of them. Right now they were holding Fletcher's arms while Sam rifled through the new boy's backpack, looking for money. Surprisingly, Fletcher wasn't protesting. In fact, Jimmy swore he saw a small smile on Fletcher's face as he stared down at the ground.

Sam dropped the bag when he saw Jim and Mike approaching. He signaled Jason and Ricky to let Fletcher go. It wasn't because he was afraid of Jim and Mike. He thought of the beating he would get from his father if he got another detention. He still had bruises from the last time the school sent a note home about his behavior. He hid the marks well.

"What's going on, Sammy boy? Looks like a robbery in progress. Not a nice way to welcome a new student," said Mike.

"Nothing's going on, butthead. 'Humpy' here is lending me a little money. Ain't ya, Humps? I'm trying to make the little guy feel welcome to good old Stockton Elementary. I'm like a one-man Welcome Wagon," Sam said with a smirk on his face. So take your girlfriend 'Prim Jim', and get outta here".

Samuel Newman was the biggest boy in 6th grade because he had stayed back two years. His greasy black hair came down to his shoulders, and covered half his face. He wore his jeans so low that at least three inches of his underwear showed. Some days he wore his pajama bottoms to school. Sam thought the piercing in his nose, lip, and ears made him look tough. He didn't care it repulsed people; in fact he liked it that it did. It was one way to get noticed even if it was negative attention. He was sent to the principal's office so many times about his appearance that the faculty finally gave up. They had written to his parents too many times and it did no good. Teachers had a job to do in educating students and didn't need to take on some parent's responsibilities of raising their children. Kids like Sam added an extra burden, and it was unfair to the students who were there to learn.

Ignoring Sam's name calling, Jim said, "We're not here to start something, Newman. Maybe we're here to stop something."

"Nobody invited you to stick your noses in my business so take your little goody two-shoes selves outta here." Sam smiled, but it was more like an evil grin. Ricky and Jason giggled. "And take Humpy with you. He's too small for my team."

"Team?" laughed Mike. "What's the name of this little team . . . The Losers? Let me guess your team colors . . . pink?" Sam would have pitched into Mike, but he spotted the playground monitor watching them.

Jimmy invited Fletcher to play some kickball before recess was over. "Good idea," chimed in Sam. The three of you can hold hands and skip away. We'd join you but I'd rather play 'kick stones' . . . at Mike's head. It's more of a manly game, one that the prison guard over there would have a cow over."

Without a word, Fletcher picked up his bag and left with Jimmy and Mike. As they walked, the boys again warned Fletcher about Sam. "He's one bad dude," said Mike. I hear he's maybe into drugs; pot I'm sure of. It was found in his locker when a surprise search was made. He was suspended for two weeks on that charge, but what good is that? He probably enjoyed it; sitting home and lighting up. Oh, by the way, my name is Mike Decker and that's Jimmy Pittenger. We're in Mr. Libby's 6th grade class. What's your name? I'm sure it's not Humpy."

"Nice to meet you, guys. I'm Fletcher and in the fifth grade."

"Where did you live before coming to Stockton?" asked Jimmy. "I'm kinda new here myself having moved from Indiana just a few years ago. I like it here, and I think you will, too. You just happened to meet the wrong guy right off the bat. I was lucky because I met Mike the first day we arrived in town. He lives next door to me and we're the same age."

"Cool," said Fletcher. Just then the bell rang to go back inside. "Guess it's too late for some kickball. I'll catch you later, guys."

As they watched Fletcher run to catch up to his class, Jimmy said, "That's odd."

"What's odd?"

"He never answered my question about where he came from."

"You didn't give him a chance. You blabbed all about your move to here," said Mike.

"I got the feeling he avoided giving an answer,"

"Oh brother, here we go again with your intuitions and suspicions.

"We'll ask him the next time we see him. No biggie."

"Yeah, next time."

CHAPTER TWO

The house was empty when Sam got home from school except for Spunky, the family dog. Sam gave the animal a hard kick that sent him flying across the kitchen floor with a yelp. The boy couldn't understand why Spunky still got excited to see him since all he did was abuse the pet every chance he got. Dogs are stupid, he thought.

Sam was glad no one was around; it gave him a chance to grab a few bucks from the jar on top of the fridge. With that money and some from his younger sister's bank, he should have just enough to buy some pot from his main source, Eddie. He grinned at the thought of robbing Erin the brat. His parents spoiled her rotten but they couldn't stand having him around. His mother couldn't care less where he went or what he did just as long as he was out of sight. As far as his father went, the old man never paid him any attention. It would be nice if he took him fishing, or to a ballgame. Yeah, like that's gonna happen. The only time he noticed Sam was to whip him for the smallest thing. It killed Sam to be forced to make a Mother's Day or a Father's Day card at school. He would rip them up into confetti and throw the pieces up into the air before he got home.

He'd get more money tomorrow, too, from that red-headed freak when Jimmy and Mike weren't around. Just thinking about those two made Sam fume. 'Maybe I can't get them at school, but I know where they live', he thought. And it was about time he taught them a lesson; a lesson so bad they'd never dare interfere with him again. For now, it was time to go into town and find Eddie. Screw doing any homework.

When Jimmy and Mike walked into the Pittenger's kitchen after school, Jimmy's mother, Eileen, greeted them with a smile and home-made blueberry muffins fresh out of the oven. "Now THIS is why I like coming to your house," said Mike with a mouthful of muffin garbling his words.

"Mike, slow down. I couldn't make out anything you just said, and you're spitting crumbs at me like bullets from a machine gun." Mike laughed, causing even bigger hunks of muffin to fly through the air.

"Oops, sorry Jim. You know how I do love to eat, especially blueberry muffins. I'm starving; the lunch today at school stunk."

"I didn't see where that stopped you from eating it, though. You cleaned your plate so good that I bet the cook in the kitchen didn't even have to wash it."

"Yeah, well that's because my stomach said I was hungry, but my taste buds told me it was gross. It didn't fill my discerning appetite."

"Discerning? Wow, that's a big word for you, Mike. However, it doesn't fit you because you'll eat anything and everything. Maybe you should cut back a little. Your chubbiness is getting a bit chubbier."

"I'm not chubby. You're too skinny. Maybe you should eat more and get a solid body like mine, Slim Jim."

Eileen laughed as she listened to the two boys. They made a good combo since day one of meeting each other. When Jimmy's dog, Laddie, heard the voices in the kitchen he came running from the living room with Mike's dog, Liberty, behind him. Liberty stood on her hind legs to give Mike kisses. "Are you happy to see me, girl, or the crumbs on my face?" laughed Mike with delight.

"Thanks for letting me stay until my mother gets home. I'm sure glad to find Liberty here, too. Nice surprise. I miss the furry gal when I'm away too long," said Mike.

"You're quite welcome, Mike. Anytime. Caroline didn't want to leave Liberty home alone so she brought him over here to keep Laddie company while she and Abigail went shopping." Mike's mother, Adele, was the school librarian, and didn't get home until around four o'clock. Caroline and Abigail were the same age and in their freshman year of high school. "So how was school today, guys? Any homework?"

"We have a little math and some English. I promised Mike to help him, especially with the English. We should be done in no time. Oh, and we met a new kid today. His name is Fletcher but that's about all we do know."

"I'm surprised that's all you know", said Eileen. "I always said you'd make a good reporter someday because of the way you always ask the four important questions; who, what, where, and when."

"Yeah," laughed Jimmy. "I'll get right on it tomorrow."

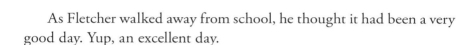

As Fletcher walked away from school, he thought it had been a very good day. Yup, an excellent day.

CHAPTER THREE

The next day was Friday and Mike and Jim couldn't wait for the weekend, plus the fact that no homework was given on the last day of the week which left them two days to have fun. Before lunch, they had to go to the auditorium to listen to a doctor give a short lecture on marijuana and the effects it has on the brain of adolescents.

Principal Robinson introduced Dr. Robert Lorch to the student body. Dr. Lorch thanked the principal and the teaching staff for having him as a guest speaker. "I'll try to be short and not toooo boring." There were scattered giggles heard from the students.

"As you know there is a lot of debate about smoking 'pot' . . . some say what's the big deal?, while others are strictly against it. Except for a few states, smoking marijuana is against the law. So if you do smoke it in this state, it's breaking the law, and that not a smart thing to do. That's one reason not to smoke, but I'm not here to talk about the legal system. I'm here today to tell you what research has discovered when kids around fourteen years old and younger use the drug. And it **is** a drug.

"The University of Maryland used your age group for their study because your brain is not fully developed yet. The scientists used adolescent mice to look at how marijuana use during adolescence impacted those still-developing brains. The mice were exposed to low doses of the active ingredient in marijuana for 20 days then returned to their sibling groups to continue maturing.

"When the mice reached adulthood, the researchers examined cortical oscillations, which are patterns of neuron activity in the brain, and found that the mice that had been exposed to marijuana had greatly altered the cortical oscillations and impaired cognitive abilities. If you're not sure of the word cognitive, I'll save you the trouble of looking it up (more giggles). It's the term for your learning skills—your ability to process information and to remember. Cognitive is the brain-based **skills** we need to carry out any task from the simplest to the most complex.

"These results don't bode well for teenagers who decide to dabble in drugs. The study's lead author, Sylvina Mullins Raver said, and I quote, 'The striking finding is that, even though the mice were exposed to very low drug doses, and only for a brief period during adolescence, their brain abnormalities persisted into adulthood.

"Why are teens so much more affected over the long term by using pot than adults are? The researchers did some deeper brain examinations of the mice in the study to try to figure that out. It appears that the frontal cortex of the brain is still developing during adolescence, and that is the part of the brain most affected by drugs. Put those two findings together and you end up with a teenage brain that has the potential to be permanently changed by drug use. In other words, the brain becomes 'fried' and it cannot be reversed.

"Now, I said I would keep it short so this concludes my talk. If anyone has questions, but don't want to share them here, I'll leave my business card for you by the exit, and you can get in touch with me. For those of you who have questions now, please stand and ask away."

Margie Thompson, who couldn't wait to take chemistry when she got to high school, was the first one to stand. "What is in marijuana to get a person 'high'?"

Dr. Lorch gave a big grin and joked, "Ho boy, I was afraid someone would ask that question because the answer is a 20 letter word. The technical name of the drug is tetrahydrocannabinol, but let's use the simple term . . . THC."

"Next?"

"Is pot addictive?" someone else asked.

"Yes and no. I say that because it depends on the smoker. If he or she uses it for a prolonged period of time because they can't cope with life, it is addictive. They use the drug as a crutch as a coping mechanism.

If they have a bad day, they have to smoke to medicate themselves. If they have a good day, they want to smoke pot to celebrate. They also let pot control their activities. Some examples are, instead of going to see a movie, they need to get high and go to the movie. Instead of dancing at a club, they need to get high and then go dancing. And so on. This means that they turn to the drug in order to avoid having to feel uncomfortable. This shuts down emotional growth because the person is not learning how to deal with life, deal with new situations and, learning to process their feelings in a healthy way.

"I'm afraid that's all the time left. The hands on the clock tell me it's almost your lunch period. I thank you all again for being here, and for your excellent questions."

As Jim and Mike shuffled behind the exiting line, they overheard Sam say, "What a dork. I think the good doc is a pothead himself", he snickered.

Mike couldn't help responding to Sam's rudeness. "Hey, Newman, your eyes look a little red. Now we know why you stayed back two years. Your cognitive thinking has been zonked."

Some of the students that heard this laughed at Mike's jab. "You won't think you're so smart when we go out after lunch, Decker. Speaking of lunch, all that talk about pot made me crave some munchies." Sam laughed at his own joke, but none of the students thought it funny at all.

CHAPTER FOUR

I t started to rain while the kids were eating lunch. The fifth and six graders were allowed to play in the gym. It ruined Sam's chance for getting back at Mike, not to mention harassing some of the students for money. A group of boys were playing kick ball. A lot of the girls were simply sitting on the bleachers and talking. Sam and his two buddies didn't join in playing anything. They just sat there watching and commenting on all the losers. Some of the remarks coming out of their mouths were pretty nasty. Mike and Jimmy invited Fletcher to join them in a game of 'Man from Mars'.

"I've never heard of that game", said Fletcher.

"It's quite simple", Jimmy answered. "Since there's ten of us playing, nine of us line up against the wall side by side behind an end-zone line; they're called 'earthlings'. The kid chosen to be 'the man from mars' stands in the middle of the gym.

"The earthlings chant, 'Man from Mars! Man from Mars! Will you take us to the stars?!' The Man from Mars says 'only if you have such and such a thing like brown hair, two dogs, a watch, or play football, etcetera. If you happen to have something he calls out, you run to the other side of the wall behind the end-zone. No one, including the man from mars can tag them.

"All the other 'earthlings' who did not have what the man from Mars called out run across the gym when the man from Mars calls out "Go!" They can get tagged by the man from mars while running. Anyone who gets tagged has to sit down on the floor where they were tagged and when the people that don't have what the man from Mars says again, both man from mars and the earthlings sitting may tag the people. The last earthling not sitting, other than the man from mars, is the winner and is the next man from mars. I'm not sure if I explained the game good enough, so maybe you want to watch how it's played and then join in?"

"Okay." Fletcher answered.

Fletcher didn't get to play the game because it had stopped raining, and the kids were allowed to go outside for the rest of recess. Mike asked Fletcher what he had planned for the weekend. "You're probably still unpacking from the move, right?"

"Not really. There wasn't much stuff to unpack."

"Jimmy and I usually just hang around or go hiking in the woods with our dogs. Our parents aren't big on having us play too much video games. They'd rather see us with a book in our hands than a remote", laughed Mike. "We tried to convince them that games help us with eye and hand coordination, but they didn't buy it. I don't really mind, though. We have enough fun reading comics in the tree house or hiking. We've had some real adventures doing just that. There was one big adventure that we would have missed if we had been stuck inside staring at a monitor."

Fletcher didn't ask him any questions about their big adventure, and Mike didn't offer an explanation. Later Mike thought Fletcher's lack of curiosity a little bit odd. When he mentioned it to Jimmy, his friend just shrugged his shoulders and said "Well, maybe that's a good thing because you really aren't allowed to say anything about finding Chatunga in a cave".

"Would you like to come over to my house tomorrow?" Jim said.

"Sure. That sounds great".

"Do you think your dad can give you a ride? If not, one of my parents could pick you up".

"I can walk. No problem. It'll give me a chance to see some of the area."

The bell rang to signal the students that recess was over and to go back to their classrooms. On the bus ride home later that afternoon, Jim turned to Mike with a puzzled look on his face and said, "Fletcher never asked where we live. Plus we don't have his phone number."

"Oh well", said Mike. The town's not that big. He's smart enough to ask people for directions."

"Did you happen to notice which bus he got on? That would help to let us know which part of the town he lives in, or maybe he's out in the countryside." said Jim.

"No, I didn't", replied Mike.

Jimmy stared out the bus window and after a while he said, "I still think there's something odd about Fletcher. I can't put my finger on it, but whatever it is; I hope it's a 'good odd' and nothing bad. For some reason, I like the little guy. Maybe I feel sorry for him; coming to a new school late in the year and then getting picked on by Sam."

Mike wasn't paying attention to what Jimmy was saying; he had his nose in a comic book.

CHAPTER FIVE

Mike showed up at Jimmy's house with Liberty around noon the next day. Jimmy had just finished his chores. It was the Pittengers' routine that every Saturday morning he and his sister, Abigail, would help their parents clean the house. Afterward, Jimmy's parents would usually drive to the yard sales that Fred Pittenger had looked up in the newspaper. He would circle the ones that sounded interesting, and then put them in numerical order. He was a mechanical engineer at the boat company in Groton which tended to make him methodical, even in his family life. "Doing it this way saves time and money on gas."

Fred and Eileen were leaving when Mike and Liberty came through the door. "Hi ya, Mom and Pop Pittenger. Wish you could stay longer but I know there are yard sales out there waiting for you. You wanna get there before the good stuff is sold. Which reminds me, if you see any comic books, could you snag 'em and I'll reimburse ya??"

Eileen and Fred laughed. They loved the way Mike and his sister Caroline were like part of the family and they especially got a kick out of Mike's humor. "Will do, Mike-o. Maybe we'll come across a first edition Superman," answered Fred.

"Fat chance of that, Mr. P. And even if you did, I'd have to be a billionaire to pay for it."

"Okay, we're leaving now. You boys stay out of trouble till we get back," said Eileen.

"Does that mean we can get into trouble after you get back?" laughed Mike.

"I say that mainly for Jim not to bother Abigail." She knew it was normal for brothers and sisters to argue, but still, she didn't like it. "Maybe you should tell her not to bug **me**, said Jimmy.

The boys watched Fred and Eileen back out of the driveway, and then Jimmy called for Laddie to go outside with him and Mike. Liberty was happy to see her good buddy.

Liberty would pick up a stick, and Laddie would try to catch her and take it away. It still caused a good feeling when they watched the two dogs play.

Mike had rescued Liberty when he and Jim went to spend a few days with Mike's grandmother in the northwest part of the state. The guy who owned her ran a dog fighting ring and he used Liberty one night to fight. It was her first time but he needed an extra dog in the ring. The dog they put into the ring was no match for Liberty, and she was attacked so severely that her owner thought she was dead. He threw her away at the edge of the woods on his way back home.

Mike and Jimmy happened to come upon her when they took Cowboy, who was his grandmother's dog, for a walk. Cowboy led them to where Liberty was lying unconscious and hardly breathing. At first they thought the dog was dead. One of Mike's friends came along and the boys had him go back to get Earlene, Mike's grandmother. She loaded the dog and the three boys into her car and raced to the local vet who was able to miraculously save her.

There was a happy ending to it all. Mike and Jim were able to expose the dog fighting business and take it down and put the owner in jail, who is still serving time. Mike's mother and his new step-dad let Mike bring her back home where for the first time in her life, Liberty felt grass under her paws and no heavy chain around her neck. She fit right in with the Decker family . . . the love was mutual . . . and slept with Mike every night.

Mike now said, "It looks like Fletcher is a no-show. So, what do you want to do?"

"I was thinking maybe we should go visit Chatunga. It's been a while since we saw him and he's not getting any younger," answered Jim.

"That's for sure. He must be over a hundred years old . . . even he doesn't know his exact age".

They had met Chatunga a few years ago when they became stranded in a cave high above the shoreline. He was the last living member of his tribe.

Chatunga's people had once lived in South America but migrated north. They were against human sacrifices to the sun god which some members of the tribe were involved in. The sacrificers threatened the peaceful half of the tribe with death.

It took Chatungas people many years to walk as far as Canada. When war broke out between the white man and Indians in 1754, they escaped in the canoes they had built over the years, and paddled south, hugging the east coast of the Atlantic Ocean. When they reached as far south as Connecticut, a fierce storm forced them onto the shore. They needed shelter and luck was with them . . . they glanced up and saw an opening in a cliff. It was a big cave, but still they didn't feel safe, afraid of being discovered. With primitive tools, they came up with a solution.*

Jimmy packed up some goodies which included a couple of the blueberry muffins his mother had made to take to Chatunga. Around the swamp and across the field they went with Laddie and Liberty following. After crossing the field, they took a path through the woods and up a steep tree-covered hill that would come out to a huge flat field. That's where Chatunga's secret grass-covered camouflaged trap door was located. They were too busy laughing and fooling around to be aware of someone watching and following them as they descended down into the earth.

*Secrets of the Cave by D.C. Marek

CHAPTER SIX

The boys found Chatunga sitting next to his campfire where he was chanting prayers to the Great Spirit. With each visit, the boys noticed he looked thinner and more fragile. The old Indian's face lit up when he saw Mike and Jimmy and their dogs. Laddie and Liberty trotted up to Chatunga with tails wagging and proceeded to give him kisses on his cheeks. "I am happy to see you, too, brother dogs," laughed Chatunga. "Now I have a clean face."

Jimmy pulled out apples, oranges, a couple bananas besides the muffins from his backpack . . . and a strawberry flavored yogurt. "What's this food you call yogurt?" asked Chatunga.

"Try it. I think you'll like it. It's made from goat's milk. Very good for you."

Chatunga took the container and a plastic spoon from Jimmy. With caution he tasted this new food. The texture was strange, but the taste was delicious.

After a few bites, he smiled. "This milk from the goat is very pleasing. Thank you."

"You're very welcome," said Mike. Ya gotta keep up your strength."

"I already feel very good after eating this strange food you call yogurt," laughed Chatunga. How could he tell these boys that his journey into the spirit world was coming soon and no matter what the nourishment was, he could not become stronger? Instead he said, "Mike and Jim, you are growing into fine young men. You are now at the age that you have to decide which path in life you will take."

"Jimbo will probably take the road to the White House seeing how he likes to read about stuffy politics and presidents. I'll probably be the gardener," laughed Mike.

"I'm not talking about your choice of jobs," smiled Chatunga. "I am speaking of the kind of people you are inside. Outwardly, being a gardener is not lowly, Mike. It is an honorable job. You are working for and with the Creator when you take care of his world.

"There are two roads; one is called the Red Road, which is very sacred. It is a good road. The other one is called the Black Road . . . . it is the bad choice. If you walk on the imaginary Red Road, you will live an honorable and truthful life with integrity. If you live a humble, honest and giving life, it will keep you on the Red Road. Truth is like the wind; you can't see it, but you can see the effect it has. At times, it can be hard to walk this Road, but never give up."

"What's the Black Road like? Just the name is scary," said Mike.

"Yes, it is scary. Not a road you want to travel. It is full of lies and hatred. The white men who attacked me and my friend Azumboa were riding on the Black Road."

"Wow, I don't want to be on **that** Road," said Mike. "There's a boy in our class who is definitely walking it. I want the good road, the Red Road."

Chatunga smiled and assured Mike he was already on it. However, he warned the boys that life could tempt them to stray off it. But they were to get right back on the Red Road which one day would lead them to a reward from the good Father in Heaven.

Jimmy told Chatunga about Sam Newman's walk on the Black Road. "He is nothing but a bully, tormenting and picking on just about everyone." Chatunga knew all too well about bullying. It led to his best friend Azumboa's death.

Their tribe had agreed to let the two boys attend the white man's school if they were careful about not being followed to or from the cave.

They loved their teacher who taught them how to read and write. She gave them English names to help them fit in . . . she named Azumboa, Samuel and Chatunga, Joseph and gave them a Bible. But still, a lot of the students hated them and made fun of their clothes, their speech, and took advantage of the two boys' shyness. The father of the biggest and worst bully tracked them down one night when Chatunga and Azumboa were out hunting. They ran and tried to hide, but the white man spotted Azumboa and shot him. Chatunga had to lie in the grass, hiding and not being able to go to his best friend's side to try to help him until the man rode away. So yes, Chatunga knew about the evilness of bullying.

As Jim and Mike prepared to leave, Chatunga asked them a favor. "Would you please ask your fathers if they could come see me in seven days?"

"Of course they will come," said Jimmy. "Is something wrong?"

Chatunga didn't want to lie to the boys, so he didn't answer Jim's question directly. Instead he said, "It's been a while and time for a visit."

The old man gave the dogs final scratches behind their ears, and then stood up to give the boys a hug good-bye. Chatunga was now much thinner, and Jim could feel his bones under the buckskin shirt. They promised they would be back soon bearing more yogurt, they laughed. As they turned to walk back up the stairs, they did not see the tears in Chatunga's eyes.

When they got up and out of the cave, Jim stopped and turned to Mike. "I think something is wrong. Did you feel how tight Chatunga hugged us good-bye?"

"Of course I did, Silly. I was there. Maybe he was just overly grateful for the yogurt." Mike tried to make a joke of it, but deep down he was worried.

The person who had followed the boys was still hiding behind a tree. He waited until Mike and Jim were out of sight, and then he walked to where he saw them open the grass-covered trap door.

CHAPTER SEVEN

O n Monday, Mr. Libby announced that for the next two weeks the students would be studying Native American Indians. "At the end of the two weeks we will practice putting on a play for the whole school. In the meantime, your assignment will be to make a diorama—a scene—of an Indian village. That'll be due next Monday. You can either make it from a shoe box, or on a flat piece of board. I'll make a list on the blackboard of the materials you might need. If you want help, that's what I'm here for," he smiled. "Also, the internet will be of help. I'll make a list of books you can read on-line. If you decide to make a book report, it'll be extra credit."

"This is going to be so cool, Jim." Mike said as they were eating lunch. Then he whispered, "Wish we could bring Chatunga to class for show-and-tell."

Sam piped up from the other end of the table, "Cool? I think it's stupid. I ain't doing it. Who cares about Indians? The white man put them in their place. We're the superior guys. If ya ain't white, you're not right, I say."

Mike jumped up and was about to attack Sam for making such a stupid remark. Jimmy grabbed him by the back of his shirt and told him to sit down. "Mike, you know he is ignorant and cruel. Ignore him. Let Mr. Libby handle him."

"I can't help it, Jim. I don't know a lot of history like you do, but I do know how cruel the Indians were treated. We wiped out whole villages, including women, babies and old people and stole their land. I could go on and on about what was done to them, but it's disgusting and it makes me mad."

"I hear ya, Mike. Maybe Sam will learn something in the next two weeks, like a little compassion . . . but I doubt it very much."

"Hey, Newman. Stay away from me at recess. I'm not gonna put up with your stupidity." Sam paid Mike no attention; he was busy taking food off other student's trays. What he didn't eat, he threw at them and laughed.

After lunch, Mike and Jimmy spotted Fletcher standing alone on the school grounds. They walked over to him and Jimmy spoke first. "Hi, Fletch. Sorry you didn't make it to my house on Saturday."

"Me, too," answered Fletcher. "Maybe we can get together next week-end. That's if you still want to."

"Sure, that would be good. I was thinking we could take a hike or something."

"Sounds good," said Fletcher.

"I'll give you my phone number and write my address down for you."

"I don't have phone service yet. But, your address would help," answered Fletcher.

The three boys spent the rest of the time talking. They asked Fletcher what movies he had seen lately, and what his favorite TV shows were. Their questions made Fletcher visibly uncomfortable. His only response was, "I really don't go to movies and stuff".

The boys didn't push it. They thought maybe his parents were very strict and they didn't want to embarrass the boy.

The bell rang to signal that recess was over. While lined up and waiting to go inside, Mike remarked, "That little dude is one strange amigo. No movies, no TV. What planet does he live on?"

"I agree. We just can't seem to get straight answers from him," answered Jimmy.

After school, the boys biked into town to see what the Stockton Public Library had for books on Indians. They were happy to find the library had a good selection on the subject. Mike picked 'Sees Behind Trees' by Michael Dorris, and Jimmy checked out 'Black Elk's Vision' by S.D. Nelson.

When they returned to Jimmy's house, they grabbed some snacks and took the books up to Jim's tree house. After a while Mike commented how interesting his book was. "This is as good as my comic books," he laughed, spitting out crumbs of Pringles.

Jimmy looked up and asked him to please swallow his food before trying to talk. "Just saying," replied Mike after gulping his soft drink.

Time flew by and before they knew it, Jimmy's mother called up to the boys to tell Mike his sister called and it was time to go home. As he climbed down the ladder he called up to Jimmy, "See you tomorrow, Chief Prancing Pittenger."

"Okay, Eats Like Buffalo, Jim laughed.

Since Sam really had to no friends to partner up with on the Indian project, he made up his mind to not even try. Instead, he went to his bedroom, tore up the teacher's notes, and cranked up his heavy metal and was just about to light up a joint when his mother came barging through the door.

"Turn that noise down!" she screamed at him. "And what's that in your hand?"

"Nothing," he yelled back and jumped off the bed, pushed her aside and ran down the stairs. He slammed the front door as he went out.

'Good riddance', Mrs. Newman thought. 'I wish he'd never come back. He's been nothing but trouble since he could walk; pulling off the wings of butterflies, almost drowning the family kitten, shooting birds and chipmunks with his BB gun; not to mention pushing Erin down a whole flight of stairs causing a broken arm. Erin is such a sweet girl; I don't know where we went wrong with Sam. Sometimes he scares me. The older he gets, the more violent he gets. And I'm getting tired of other parents calling to complain about their children getting abused by Sam. He's headed toward one of those tough reformatory camps if it keeps up.' She sat down on Sam's bed and wept.

CHAPTER EIGHT

The rest of the school week went by uneventfully, except for one serious incident. On the bus ride home on Wednesday, Sam called Diane Jenkins fat; a regular bubble butt. He said it loudly enough so that all the students heard him and laughed which made him say some more terrible things just for the laughs. Diane went home in tears and tried to swallow a whole bunch of pills, but thankfully her mother found her in time and called 911. The ER doctor was able to save her by pumping the drugs out of her stomach. She later told her parents she never wanted to go back to school. When she finally told them why she tried to end her life, they called the school to report Sam's cruelty against their daughter. The only thing the principal could do was suspend Sam for the rest of the week since he didn't actually put the pills into Diane's mouth. But he may as well have done so. The news of what he had done to cause Diane to almost die didn't faze Sam at all. In fact, he thought she was stupid and the planet would be better off without her.

Sam didn't mind the suspension. He could lie around and goof off which included sneaking in a few war games on his X-box . . . a regular mini vacation while the poor suckers in school worked their little pea brains off. It also gave him time to let the bruises heal from the beating his father gave him after the school called to report what Sam had done. If anything bothered Sam at all it was the fact he might stay back another year, making it the third time. He laughed at the idea he might be stuck in 6th grade until he was old enough to quit school and get out of this podunk town. (Little did Sam know, but he used a Natick Indian word for 'swampy place' which we use as a slang word for a small town).

Jim liked his bedroom the first day he saw it. He had been bummed out about leaving Indiana, but when his father showed him the room that would be his, he was amazed. The double glass doors opened up onto a deck where he could see the Atlantic Ocean in the distance. The site blew him away because he had never seen the sea before. The added bonus was a telescope mounted to the railing. He loved watching the various boats out on the water. On hot summer nights, Jimmy left the double doors open to feel the ocean breeze and smell the salt air that it brought in. Jimmy also like the nautical-themed wallpaper his father had hung. His framed pictures of some of the U.S. Presidents looked good on the walls.

Mike's bedroom had bright colors; each of the four walls painted a different primary color: red, green, yellow, and blue. Posters of super heroes such as Spiderman, Batman, and Superman hung on his walls. Whereas Jimmy had book cases neatly filled with books, Mike had stacks of comic books on the floor. Mike thought his own room much cooler than Jimmy's.

The biggest difference in the two boys' bedrooms was Mike's untidiness and Jimmy's neatness.

Sometimes it was hard to walk across Mike's room without stepping or tripping on something. Mike's dirty clothes rarely hit the hamper. Jimmy couldn't imagine how a pair of Sam's underwear landed on the top of a curtain rod. He didn't ask. He never judged Mike's habits. Jimmy figured a person's bedroom was the only place one could call truly his own. And if this was what made Mike happy, so be it. However, Jim once did offer to help Mike tidy up his room.

"What's wrong with my room? I know where everything is, so don't touch a thing. Geez Jimbo, you're starting to sound like Caroline or my mother." Jimmy knew that was a lie about knowing where everything was because he more than once saw Mike digging to find something, which caused an even bigger mess.

Most of the time they did their projects at Jimmy's where there was more room to work. Right now they were working on their Indian dioramas.

They had gone to the local hobby shop to buy the materials, including miniature Indians and horses. While working on the villages, Jimmy said "Do you know the Indian name for Connecticut, Mike?"

"Don't know," replied Mike while concentrating on making a teepee. "Taxalot? Get it . . . Tax-A-Lot?" He laughed at his own joke. He had often heard his mother and the Commander complain about the high cost of living and high taxes.

"Well I know." said Jimmy. "Quinnetukqut." It means 'Long River' and refers to the Connecticut River running through Hartford.

"And you know this how?"

"Connecticut is a weird name for a state so I looked it up on the internet to see how it got its name. When I moved to here from Indiana, I thought I'd never learn how to spell Connecticut. I had to break it down into three words . . . connect I cut. But after reading the spelling of the original Indian name, Connecticut seems a lot easier."

"That's for sure," agreed Mike as he tried to get two of his fingers unstuck from the glue, which by now were orange from eating from a box of Cheez-Its.

"I'll tell you something else I bet you don't know," continued Jimmy.

"There are a lot of things that you know and I don't, Bookhead. We're here to have fun building villages, not to be bored by facts." Mike let out a huge pretend yawn.

Jimmy ignored Mike's remarks and continued, "Our U.S. Constitution is modeled after the political system of the Iroquois."

"You're right. I didn't know that. If you keep telling me so many facts, I might have to wrap duct tape around my brain so it won't explode."

"Okay, Mike. You're getting tired and stupid. Let's call it quits for tonight. And you better pick the crumbs from the middle of your camp unless they're already dried into the glue."

Fletcher spent the hours before bedtime alone in his room writing in a large ledger. He scowled at the words he recorded.

CHAPTER NINE

The next day at school Jimmy asked Mike if he told his step-dad about Chatunga wanting to see him on Saturday. "Yes, I did and yes, he will. He said he'd get in touch with your father to see what time would be good."

"I'm really curious what it's all about. Maybe we can go see Chatunga after they have their little powwow."

Mike laughed. "Geeze, Jimbo, I think all this Indian stuff we have to do is getting to you. You're starting to talk like one using words like powwow and stuff."

"Who me? You talking to me, Kimosabe??" laughed Jimmy.

"I was going to suggest we go to the movies on Sunday to see 'Lone Ranger', but now I'm thinking it might be a bad idea," said Mike. "It could send you over the edge and you'd want to live in a teepee in your backyard wearing a loin cloth and feathers stuck in your hair."

"That might be cool," laughed Jimmy. "I've always loved the Native American culture and wished sometimes that I could live on a real reservation."

"See what I mean? You're starting to talk like me, and that's kinda scary."

"Enough joking around. I say we go to the movies on Sunday."

"Sounds like a plan." said Mike. "Afterward we could work on our lines for the play. I'm nervous about having to stand on the stage in front of an audience. Show-biz can be tough."

"You only have about four lines to memorize, and in case you forget them, Mr. Libby is letting us put our lines on a card to glance at. You talk like you're Johnny Depp, or someone."

"Yeah, well I just don't like it. But I might sign autographs if asked," replied Mike

Jimmy just shook his head. "You're a piece of work. Sometimes I don't know if you're kidding or you're serious."

The title of the play was 'How the Animals Taught a Young Brave Truth'. It was the story of a twelve-year old boy named 'Swift As Fox' of the Pequot tribe. His name was given to him because he was a fast runner, and he won all the races in competitions with his fellow braves. This made Swift as Fox boastful and full of pride which annoyed some members of his tribe. Under the guidance of the tribal Medicine Man, the elders sent him away to live alone in the forest for three days to learn wisdom and humility from Mother Earth and the animals.

As the boy sat under a tree, the first animal to approach him was the wolf since he was regarded as a teacher of loyalty. The wolf ran in packs which signified loyalty to family and friends. "You must not think yourself above your fellow braves."

The deer taught him about compassion, generosity and unconditional love. The hunters took only what was needed for the tribe, and always offered up a prayer of thanks to the Great Spirit after taking the life of an animal. By hunting only what was necessary for the tribe, the deer told Swift As Fox it represented living for the greater good—not selfishly.

Many more animals came and each one spoke of courage, protection, and consideration of each other. Even the snake slithered up to Swift As Fox to explain how the shedding of his skin symbolized change and letting go of old habits.

Jimmy was cast as the wolf, and Mike as the deer. "I wish Sam would take part in the play," said Mike. "He'd make a perfect snake."

"Not really," said Jimmy. "The snake represents shedding of old habits and I can't see that happening in Sam's life. Speaking of the big bully, I wonder if he'll come back to school next week meaner than ever."

If the boys could see Sam at that moment, Jimmy's question would be answered. And it wasn't a good answer. Sam was staring at the TV screen like a zombie while he fantasized about getting rid of Mike and

Jimmy . . . even that creep Fletcher. Well, maybe not Fletcher. He kinda liked the little guy and he would be an easy mark; that is, if Decker and Pittenger weren't around to stop him.

At that exact moment, a cold chill passed through Fletcher's body.

CHAPTER TEN

Mike showed up at Jim's house Friday night after supper. He was carrying his sleeping bag under his arm. "Where's Liberty?" said Jimmy.

"Caroline and Abigail plan to take her and Laddie tomorrow for a make-over at the doggie beauty parlor or whatever it's called. Nobody informed you of their plans?"

"No. She should have asked me first," fumed Jimmy. "Laddie is MY dog. Not hers!" He had been a Christmas gift from Jimmy's parents a few years ago. "And he better not come back smelling like perfume. Lad is fine just the way he is." Jimmy was right; Laddie's mother was a pure bred collie, and his father was a black Springer spaniel, resulting in the puppies to be a black and white color. Laddie had a 'bib'of white, four white paws and a coat of black. A thin strip of white ran down to his white muzzle. He was a beautiful and gentle dog.

Just then Abigail walked into the kitchen with Laddie on a leash. "I assume blabber mouth Mike filled you in about taking Laddie and Liberty to the 'Viva La Pooch Pet Salon' I'm staying over with Caroline tonight with Laddie because the appointment is set for early tomorrow morning. Mom said he was starting to smell too 'doggie-ish."

"That's because he **IS** a dog. The smellier dogs are, the more they like it. I'm warning you, Abigail, Laddie better not come back looking like a poodle and smelling like a bimbo."

Abigail made a mocking ha-ha laugh, and Jimmy swore her last words going out the door were something about a tutu. "Sisters! They can make our lives miserable, Mike."

"You can say that again, pal. Least we're rid of them for the night. I hate to see our dogs go through that kinda torture, but when they come home after the beauty treatment we can take them over to the swamp; let 'em roll around in the mud to get the stink off."

Mike's dog, Liberty, was tan and white and had short hair with a tail that curled. She was mainly terrier mixed with other unknown breeds. Now that she had a loving home and was well taken care of, she emerged into a beautiful dog. When Mike laid his eyes on her for the very first time, Liberty's fur was dirty and matted; and her claws were painfully long. She was so thin that it broke his heart to look at her. With a good diet and exercise, she gained weight and strength. Mike said that Liberty was his favorite breed of dog . . . it was called 'Rescued'.

"Let's go to the tree house while there's still plenty of light left," suggested Jimmy. "Did you bring the book you'll be writing a report on?"

"Yep, indeed I did." That was a half-truth statement. Mike had the book alright, but he also had a comic book hidden inside it. "Are you bringing any dessert left over from supper?"

"Sure. I'm stuffed, but there's a piece of apple pie left that you can have. I'm not putting ice cream on it, though. You'll make enough mess with just the pie."

They read (or at least Jimmy did) until the sun was starting to set in the west. The tree frogs started making a racket in the nearby swamp. "Listen to that cacophony, will ya," said Jim. He liked using big words around Mike just to irritate him.

"I never heard of a cacophony. Is it like a saxophone? Nobody lives close enough for us to hear music."

"Cacophony means a bunch of loud unconnected sounds. The male tree frogs are making the noise to attract a mate. Maybe you should try it to attract Jennie Smith," teased Jimmy.

"Why you, I oughta . . ." responded Mike with his fist in the air. "I don't like Jennie. Stop saying that I do."

"Simmer down, Frog Boy," laughed Jim. "The more you deny it, the more I believe you do have a crush on her."

"Okay, that's it. I'm going in the house to get the ice cream that you denied me on the piece of pie."

After the two boys went into the house, Sam stood for a few moments in the shadows grinning. He had been hiding near the tree house and heard what Jimmy had said about Jennie Smith. "So, little Mikey's got a thing for Jennie. I'll just have to do something about that. I know where she lives. In fact, I think I'll pedal on over to her house right now and do a little spying through her bedroom window."

Under the cover of darkness, Sam climbed a tree that stood in back of Jennie's house. A light came on in one of the upstairs windows, and he lucked out. It was Jennie's bedroom. He could see her changing into her blue pajamas. "Perfect", he thought to himself. After the bedroom light went off, Sam climbed down from the tree. "Now to write a little love note when I get back home to tell Jennie how adorable her pajamas are . . . and I'll sign it 'Michael Decker' . . . make it really formal. Maybe I'll even add a few X's and O's. It'll be in her desk on Monday morning . . . Mwahahahahahaha"

CHAPTER ELEVEN

Fred and Eileen were in the living room watching TV when the two boys filled huge bowls with ice cream to take up to Jimmy's room to play an NBA basketball game on Xbox. Jimmy wasn't allowed to have any of the bloody war games that most of his friends played. "Geeze, I wish they stop treating me like a baby or something," said Jim as he started up the game.

Jimmy won the first game, and Mike the second one. They decided to call it quits at the tie. "We should have played two out of three. I probably would have beaten you," said Mike.

"Yeah, yeah, whatever," answered Jim. "I've got to get a new game; I'm bored with this one. Maybe we should work on our Indian project. We're almost done . . . just a few more tweaks to go on the villages. After that we can finish reading our books. I'm going to write a book report for the extra credit. Are you?"

"Jim, I'll be lucky if I can finish reading my book. Maybe you can write a report for me?"

"I don't think so. You could have read the whole book by now if you hadn't wasted time reading the comic books you hid inside the book."

'Boy, you just can't put anything over on him', thought Mike. He was a little embarrassed, but not too much.

"That reminds me, we have to ask our mothers for help on our costumes. If Mom could help me with the wolf's ears and tail, I think I'll just wear grey pants and shirt with some kind of fake fur glued to them. She is an expert sewer so maybe she can help you with the deer costume if your mom is too busy." continued Jimmy.

"I have a pair of antlers that I found in the woods one winter. Wonder if I could strap them onto the top of my head. Only problem is they weigh a ton."

Jimmy laughed at the vision of big antlers on Mike's head causing him to lose his balance and wipe out half the players, or rip the stage curtain. "Maybe you should see if we can find you a set of fake antlers at the novelty store. You know, the kind people think it's funny to put on their dogs at Christmas."

"Yeah, you're probably right, Jimbo. Hey, you gave me an idea when you said you're wearing gray for the wolf. I'll wear brown clothes and black mittens for hooves for my deer."

"Sounds good, Mike, but maybe we should run our ideas past Mr. Libby. He might have something better to offer."

After they completed their Indian villages, they decided to go to bed. It was going to be a busy day and they had to get up early. They talked for a while in the dark. Just as Jimmy was dozing off, Mike said, "Pssst, you asleep, Jim?"

"Just about. Go to sleep, Mike."

"I was just thinking about Zebulon. Have you had any visits from him lately?"

Zebulon Seeley was an American Revolutionary soldier. His grandfather had built the house the Pittengers now lived in. He appeared one night as a ghost during Christmas vacation while Mike was sleeping over at Jimmy's. He was there to ask for the boys' help in solving a murder that he was innocent of. He had gotten their attention by rolling Jimmy's baseball across the floor in the dark.

"Nope, I haven't seen him since he was proven not guilty and passed over to the 'other side' to be with his parents."

"I kinda miss him. I just hope he's happy and at peace," yawned Mike.

A few minutes later there was a sound in the dark room. Jimmy put his bedside light on to see what Mike was doing. But Mike was asleep. He glanced down and there was his Willie Mays baseball on the floor. Jimmy smiled and put out the light. 'Good night, Zeb' he whispered in the darkness.

**Haunted Holidays, A Revolutionary Christmas

CHAPTER TWELVE

Mike dreamed of being in school wearing only his underwear. He was trying to give a book report on a book he had never read. Sam was in the back of the classroom taunting him while the class laughed. Jimmy stood up and yelled, "I told you not to read comic books!!" Mike stood there in front of the class feeling humiliated. The classroom door opened and Fletcher walked in. The only word he spoke as he pointed a finger at Mike was 'Beware'.

"Mike! Mike! Wake up. You're having a bad dream."

Mike opened his eyes to see Jimmy standing over him, shaking him. "Phew, I'll say. Hey, give me my library book. I gotta read it!"

"Why the sudden change? Last night you said you weren't going to read it."

"I don't want to be standing in my underwear if Mr. Libby calls on me."

Jimmy laughed. "C'mon, Mike. Wake up. You're not making any sense. It's time to get up"

Mike told Jimmy about his nightmare. "What was scarier than me half naked was Fletcher saying 'Beware'. It was like a warning of some kind; but a warning about what?"

"Probably nothing; just a part of the dream and nothing more." said Jimmy.

"Easy for you to say. You weren't there. You didn't see the look on his face."

"Forget about Fletcher. I have the feeling he doesn't want anything to do with us. If he did, he would have made solid plans to come over here or have us go to his house. We still don't even know where he lives.

"Get up and don't forget to dress. I don't want my mom to see you in your underwear." laughed Jim.

The boys could smell bacon frying as they walked into the kitchen. Fred was reading the newspaper at the table. "Good morning, Geronimo and Crazy Horse," he said.

"Very funny, Dad, but they were out west. We're studying about the Indians around this area."

"What have you learned?" said Fred.

"A lot. Mike and I plan to go see Chatunga after you and Mr. Dixon get back. We want to share with him what we've learned so far and ask him if he has anything to add."

"Sounds good to me. Maybe he can teach you guys how to do a rain dance to share with your classmates," commented Fred absent-mindedly as he turned a page of his newspaper.

"Dad, your sense of humor is getting dryer by the day." said Jim. Mike couldn't help but giggle. He thought Fred Pittenger was always saying something funny even though he looked like a very serious person with his black rimmed glasses and all. That made everything he said funnier.

Eileen flipped four eggs in the skillet and then turned to face the boys sitting at the table. "Jim, butter the toast. Mike, you can set the table if you would, please. After you eat, Jim, make your bed and pick up your room. This Saturday you don't have to do the usual cleaning. Your father is going over to Mike's house to speak with Tom before going to see Chatunga. Since you'll be going to see him later, I want to make a gift basket for him. Plus, I have to do some baking for tomorrow's bake sale at the church. Tag sales will have to wait till next week."

"There are no good listings anyway," said Fred. "But here's something interesting. It says that the police were called out to a complaint about someone living in the old Killmer mansion at the edge of town. That place has been empty for years."

"What's so interesting about that?" asked Eileen. "Probably just kids hanging out. Simple case of trespassing."

"They found a backpack with school papers inside. The name on them was Fletcher, no last name. What would a young kid be doing in that spooky house?"

Jimmy and Mike's looked at each other with wide eyes. "Dad, there's a new boy in the fifth grade. His name is Fletcher. I don't know his last name because he never told me and Mike what it is. He was evasive when we asked anything personal."

"I'll make a phone call to the police. They can question the teacher or the principal. They will have all his information on record. This sounds to me like it could be a case of an abandoned kid."

When Fred got off the phone with the police, he came back into the kitchen with a puzzled look on his face. Mike, with a mouthful of toast, asked what the police said.

"They were one jump ahead of me. They had already questioned school officials. The teacher and staff said they had never heard of a student named Fletcher. Are you boys sure you got his name and class right?"

"Yes, Dad. We hung out with him a couple times at recess. He has red hair, kinda thin, and has a humped back. I hate to say this, but you can ask Sam Newman . . . he was bullying Fletcher the day we met him."

"Want to hear something else weird?" said Fred. "The cops told me that the house is full of dust and cobwebs, but not one fingerprint was found."

"Well, whoever called in the complaint must have seen Fletcher go in or out of the house, right?" asked Mike.

"The call was traced to your bully pal, Sam Newman. He said he happened to see Fletcher come out from the house. If you ask me, I think he was just trying to get the kid in trouble," said Fred. "If Sam is as bad as you say he is, then I think his motive was to steal copper piping or anything else he could get money for; and your friend Fletcher would get the blame later."

"I can't wait till Monday when Sam comes back to school. He's been suspended since last Wednesday. Jim and I will get the truth out of the jerk." fumed Mike.

"I don't want you boys to go near him. Let the police handle the case, or you'll be the ones facing a suspension." said Fred. "Right now, I've got to take a shower and get ready to go over to your house, Mike."

As the boys did their few chores, they talked about the Fletcher-Sam mystery. "Let's take a bike ride out to the Killmer mansion. Maybe we can find Fletcher. At least we now know where he lives or has been living," said Jimmy.

They followed through with their plan, but there was no sight of the strange red-headed boy.

Little did Mike and Jimmy know that Fletcher spotted them coming toward the mansion. He quickly ducked into some tall bushes and laid low until they passed. He, too, had things to do today. And time was running out.

CHAPTER THIRTEEN

Jimmy and Mike decided the next stop would be the novelty shop to try to find antlers for Mike. As they poked around the store, Mike became distracted looking at some gag toys. "Hey, Jimbo, look at the fake blood. Wouldn't it be cool to freak out our sisters? Bet they'd scream their heads off. Or how about this fake vomit? It looks like the real stuff . . ."

"Mike, concentrate. I don't see any antlers. Let's go ask for help." He walked up the aisle in front of Mike when he heard a loud farting sound come from behind him. "Mike! You're disgusting!"

"Haha, fooled ya," laughed Mike. It's called the Pooter. Sounds like the real thing, right? Better than a Whoopee cushion because you can put this baby in your pocket and squeeze it. I gotta buy one and squeeze it every time I walk by Caroline."

"Yeah, yeah, Clown Boy. That reminds me, did I ever tell you I don't like clowns? They creep me out." said Jimmy as they approached a store clerk. Mike wasn't sure if Jimmy was talking about real clowns, or referring to him.

The clerk led them to where the antlers were. Mike tried them on, and then pranced like a deer up to the check-out counter while squeezing the Pooter. Jimmy couldn't stop laughing. "You're cray-cray, Mike; a regular super nut."

"I'm just practicing my part in the play. And how can I be 'regular' if I'm 'super'? Those two words don't go together. Just say I'm super. Honestly, Jimbo, you better polish up on your English."

"Okay, *Super Nut*. Just pay for the antlers and your farting toy and let's go. But, I'm telling you now, don't wear the antlers on the bike ride home."

They were hungry when they reached Jim's house. Eileen cautioned them not to jump around as she had things baking in the oven. Jimmy got the mayo out, and sliced up a cucumber to make sandwiches. Mike was leery at first but after a couple bites he said, "Hey, this isn't bad." Mike was always game to try new foods. "How'd you think of putting cucumbers between bread? Next you'll be putting spinach on toast."

"I think in one of my Sherlock Holmes' stories. It's an English treat."

"I might have known you read it somewhere. Well, pip, pip, and cheerio," said Mike with a British accent as he took another bite.

The sandwiches were followed by left-over strawberry Jell-o and RediWhip. Mike took the can and squirted some of the cream into his mouth. "Don't let my mother catch you doing that." said Jimmy. Then he whispered, "Save some for me."

After they cleaned up their dishes, Jim suggested they take their books up to the tree house. "And don't sneak a comic book in it," warned Jimmy. "I know your tricks; I'll make a reader out of you yet. By the way, I've changed my mind. If you finish your book, I'll help you with writing a report. Deal?"

"Yeah, I guess so. Deal," responded Mike without much enthusiasm.

The next hour passed in silence as the boys read. Mike was relieved when Jimmy suggested they take a break and hike up to the field above the woods. Maybe their fathers would soon be coming up from Chatunga's cave, and they could find out how the visit went. Jimmy said after that, they then could go see Chatunga and give him the basket of goodies that Eileen had prepared.

Someone else was relieved, too, that they were finally coming down from the tree house. Sam Newman had been hiding and watching, wondering what they could be doing up there for so long. It had been awfully quiet. He was almost ready to leave, but luck was on his side. They were talking as they came down the ladder about going to see some guy named Cha-*tuna* or something like that. Sam would follow them once they left the yard. He had a plan that would get those two freaks off his back for good.

CHAPTER FOURTEEN

After much huffing and puffing, Fred Pittenger and Tom Dixon finally reached the top of the hilly woods. They stopped to rest a few minutes to catch their breaths. Tom spoke first. "I wonder why Chatunga wants to see us. The boys were here just a week ago, weren't they? Did Jimmy mention anything"

"Not really; only that Chatunga didn't look too well."

"Well, we know he's extremely old. If he's sick, I doubt very much he would agree to see a doctor. A hospital would be out of the question. Then again, it might not have anything to do with his health. Maybe he just plain wants adult company. I hope." said Tom thoughtfully.

The two men looked around to make sure no one was in the area before opening the trap door in the field. The stairway was dark which was unusual. Chatunga usually kept torches burning to light the stairs, especially if he expected company. They didn't want to scare the old man so they called out his name as they carefully descended down the stairs. There was no response. Tom turned on his small flashlight.

There was some light shining into the cave from the opening that overlooked the sea. It was just enough to show Chatunga lying next to the campfire which was now nothing but cold embers. It must have gone out days ago. There was an odor of death in the air.

"Oh my God," exclaimed Fred. "No wonder he didn't want the boys to come with us. Chatunga knew he was dying with only a few days to live". He choked up as he spoke.

Tom joined Fred and knelt beside the lifeless body for a moment to say a silent prayer. He helped Fred carry Chatunga into one of the wigwams where they could cover him up. The old body was pitifully light. "Be at peace, dear friend." Tom said, after they laid Chatunga on a blanket.

When Tom came out of the wigwam, he saw Fred reading something. He walked over and shined the flashlight onto the paper Fred was holding. Fred read the printed words aloud:

'To my dear friends, Tom and Fred. I am sorry you have to be the ones to find this old shell of mine. My spirit has left the body and will travel to join my families who have been waiting for me for too many years. Commander Tom, you said you would bury me in the sea as I asked when we first met. I hope you can keep that promise. Please tell Jim and Mike I love them and not to be sad. Above all tell them how much joy they brought me for the last few years of my life. All that I have is now theirs. It isn't much. Tell them to keep walking on the Red Road. With Respect, Chatunga Joseph, Last of my Tribe."

The two men sat in silence for a few minutes. Then Tom cleared his throat and said he would make all the arrangements for burial. He would mark it Top Secret with his fellow Guardsmen.

They met Jimmy and Mike coming up the hill carrying a basket. Trying to sound casual, Fred told them that Chatunga wasn't feeling well and didn't feel up to any more company today. The boys were disappointed, but said okay. Jimmy asked his father if he would take the basket back home. Since they were almost to the top of the hill, they might as well go to the field to pick apples that had fallen from Mr. Applegate's trees.

They always thought that was an appropriate name for a man who owned an apple orchard.

"Okay," said Fred. But don't be too long. And above all, do not bother Chatunga." They promised they wouldn't and would be home in a little while.

After the two men left, Mike said "Hey, we could've used the basket to put the apples in."

"I'll use my jacket like a bucket," said Jimmy. "No problemento. 'Necessity is the mother of invention' I say. That's a good quote and it's true."

The boys were disappointed that the apples weren't ripe yet. And even more disappointed that they couldn't go see Chatunga. "I hope he'll be well enough by next weekend," said Mike. "We may as well go back to your house and hang out. I wonder if the girls have brought our dogs back yet?"

"I hope so. Our dogs would rather be here with us than with Abby and Caroline, that's for sure. No sooner had Jimmy got his words out when the sky turned black. A bright bolt of lightning appeared in the sky followed by a loud clap of thunder.

"Yikes!" Mike yelled out. "I'm scared of lightning, Jim. We have to get some place where it's safe, but where? Trees surround the field; trees are a big no-no to stand under, and we'd be sitting ducks in the field."

The wind started picking up strength. Jimmy stood there thinking for a few minutes. He'd read once an old farmer's theory that when you saw lightning, start counting one thousand one, one thousand two and so on. If you got up to, let's say one-thousand five, it meant that the lightning was five miles away. In other words, each second equaled one mile, but with the speed of this storm, he wouldn't count on the theory. All he knew was they had to find some kind of cover. It wasn't that he was afraid of lightning like Mike, but he knew the danger and respected it. He read that lightning could strike from even five miles away.

Jimmy looked around when a strong gust of wind parted the branches on a bunch of pine trees, revealing what looked like an old house. Of all the times he and Mike had been up here in the field, Jimmy never noticed it before. It was closer to get to than Chatunga's cave. "Hey, Mike," he yelled over the now hurricane force of wind. "Whose house is that over there?"

Mike turned to see where Jimmy was pointing. "I forgot all about that place. The trees have grown up and blocked it. I think I'd rather take my chances under a tree than to go into that house. I've heard stories of it being haunted. No one lives there."

"Okay, you've got two choices; getting struck by lightning or scared to death by a ghost. I'll take my chances with a ghost." Jimmy ran toward the house. "C'mon Mike. Let's go!"

Mike hesitated until another big clap of thunder sounded. "Wait up for me," he yelled as he ran behind Jim.

They weren't the only two people running for shelter in the abandoned house.

CHAPTER FIFTEEN

As Jimmy and Mike pushed their way through the tightly knitted pine branches, the sky opened up and buckets of rain started falling. "Hurry up, Jim. I'm getting soaked," said Mike. "And the branches are slapping me in the face; can't you hold them back until I get through?"

"Sorry, Mike." Jimmy reached the porch stairs first. "Watch your step; most of the boards are rotted . . . . let's hope the door isn't locked."

It took a little effort, but finally the swollen door gave way and they entered the dark house. "Cripes," said Mike, "just the sound of the creaking door scares me. Sounds like something out of a scary movie. You know . . . . the kind of movie where the audience is trying to tell the actor 'don't go in there'.

"Well, there's no audience and we *are* in here," Jimmy. "So just relax while we wait out the storm. I don't think it'll last long. Let's take a seat on the floor and you can tell me what you know about this place. You've lived in this town all your life, so you must have heard something."

"Yeah, I've heard people talk and they all tell the same story. About a hundred years ago, a man named Harry Warner was building this house for his fiancé as a wedding gift. Well, wouldn't ya know it, she ups and leaves him before it's finished. Women! I tell ya."

"I don't need your personal comments, Mike. Just tell the story."

"I'm just saying. So, she broke the guy's heart and he stopped working on the house. Even left his tools right where they were and went back to his parent's house to live until he died. People who have had the nerve to come in here say they heard crying and footsteps. They claim it's Harry looking for his beloved. Personally, I wouldn't waste my tears on any woman. If I had been ole Harry, I woulda finishd the house and then I'd go out and look for another woman. Or maybe I'd just stay a bachelor and live the high life. Like they say, 'there's plenty of fish in the sea', which I never really understood what that means. I thought maybe it meant that the guy should get a pole and go fishing to help him forget."

Jimmy laughed. "It simply means that there is more than just woman in the world to fall in love with and marry. You can also apply it to women who have been jilted by a man."

"Yeah, but why call them fish?"

Jimmy shook his head and said "Never mind. Let's look around. I think this storm might last longer than I thought."

A hallway led from the small entry way where they had been sitting. There were doorways on each side of the hall, but no doors, except for one room. Jim opened that door slowly to look inside. It looked like it would have been a parlor. Or a living room as we say today. There was a fireplace, and unlike the other bare rooms, this one had two wooden chairs. They didn't look old; in fact they looked like they just came from Ikea, a furniture store that didn't exist in Harry's day.

"That's strange," said Jimmy. "Maybe some homeless person has been living here."

"If they are or were, they have pretty good taste in expensive chairs. If they can afford chairs like this, then they can afford to rent a place instead of living in this dilapidated old hou . . ."

"Quiet!" Jim interrupted. "Did you hear that?"

"Hear what? I can't hear anything over the rain," whispered Mike.

"The front door. I swear I heard it creak open." Jimmy put a finger to his lips, signaling Mike not to talk. They heard footsteps approaching and they were getting louder as they got nearer. There was no where to hide.

CHAPTER SIXTEEN

Adele and Tom Dixon were sitting at the Pittenger's kitchen table drinking coffee with Eileen and Fred. Adele had asked Caroline to stay home with Abigail and the two dogs. Tom and Fred had broken the news to their wives about the death of Chatunga. Plans had to be made and they didn't want to be interrupted by two teenage girls with two dogs. One of the subjects brought up was how to tell Jimmy and Mike.

"It'll be hard," said Eileen. "I really don't know how they'll take the news. It's Jimmy's first time dealing with the death of someone he is, or I should say was, close to."

"Same for Mike," said Adele. "The closest he came to losing anyone was when his father and I divorced. He missed his father and yet at the same time he was angry at him for moving so far away to Florida". She glanced over at Tom, "But then Tom came into our lives and has been a good father to him and Caroline. They both love Tom very much."

Tom smiled. "The feeling is quite mutual. I knew there was a reason I waited so long to get married. And I can't help thinking that Chatunga had some part in our meeting."

Eileen was happy for her friend. Adele had been a hard working single mom trying to raise two kids by herself. She did a fine job. You couldn't ask for two nicer kids than Mike and Caroline.

"Have you spoken to any of your men, Tom?" asked Fred.

"Yes, I called my Chief Petty Officer when we got back home, and told him I'd be at the base around four o'clock for a meeting. I told him to have three seamen there with him. It'll be a closed door private session. Do you want to hold the funeral for tomorrow or Monday?"

"I guess tomorrow morning" answered Fred. "Is that enough time to prepare the guys?"

"They're always prepared at a moments notice," assured Tom. "And above all, they're trustworthy. I wish Mike and Jim would get back here before I have to leave. I want to be here when you break the news to them."

"They should be home soon. Since we told them not to go to see Chatunga, what else is there to do up there? Then again, it doesn't take much to distract them and forget about time. It's such a beautiful sunny day out there. Wish it could last forever." said Fred wistfully. The two women teared up and grabbed a Kleenex from the box sitting in the middle of the table. They cried for Chatunga, but most of all they cried for Jimmy and Mike.

CHAPTER SEVENTEEN

The footsteps continued on past the living room where Mike and Jimmy were now standing flat against a wall, holding their breaths. When they were sure whoever it was had gone to the back of the house where the kitchen would have been, they opened the door, and slipped out quietly to get to the front door. Jimmy had his hand on the door knob to get outside when a voice behind them said, "Where do you think you're going?"

As they turned around, a huge flash of lightning lit up the foyer, revealing Sam Newman! He was soaking wet and his long hair was hanging partly in his face. The bright light made him look like some kind of deranged madman. "Not a nice way to greet a fellow classmate; aren't you happy to see me?" His smile sent chills through Jimmy and Mike.

Another flash of lightning revealed a shiny knife in his hand.

Mike was not only afraid, but also confused. He found his voice and asked, "How did you find us?"

"Oh, I've been keeping close watch on my two favorite nerds. I knew if I waited long enough that I'd get to catch you alone where no one was around. And now, here we are . . . together at last."

Jimmy said, "Please put that knife away. You'll get into serious trouble if you hurt us."

Sam answered, "How can I get in trouble if you're not around to talk?" Jimmy couldn't believe that Sam would go from a bully-nuisance to a killer! This can't be happening. He's just trying to scare us. On Monday he'll be back at school laughing and bragging to his buddies, Jason and Ricky, how he scared the 'you-know-what' out of us.

"Please don't be offended," Sam said with sarcasm, "but I can't stand people like you. Always got your nose in other people's business, especially my business, and everyone thinks you are so great; little heroes even. I bet your mommies tuck you into bed every night, and make you breakfast in the morning blah, blah, blah."

"So you're going to kill us because our mothers make us breakfast?" asked Mike. If Jimmy wasn't so scared, he would have laughed. Leave it to Mike, he thought.

"Shut up, you little wise-acre. You think this is funny? You think I'm joking?" snapped Sam.

"I don't think you've thought this through, Sam. There's two of us and only one of you. One of us is bound to get away. Besides, you don't want to go to jail over someone like us. We're not worth it," said Jimmy.

"Oh, but you **are** worth it; it'll make me feel real good knowing you both are off this planet. Besides, I'm a juvenile and if, and that's a big if, if I'm caught my sentence will be light. I'll be free in just a few years. So you see, I *have* thought this through. Now, get away from the door, and walk slowly toward the room with the chairs in it. I'll be right behind you so don't try to be the heroes everyone thinks you are."

The boys could hear the storm intensifying as they walked down the long hallway. "God, please send a bolt of lightning and strike Sam right now," Mike prayed silently. When they reached the doorway to the living room, Mike's prayer was answered; not by lightning, but by a forceful push that knocked Jimmy and Mike back out of the room and pulled Sam into it. The door slammed shut, followed by a boom so loud it knocked Jim and Mike to the floor and for a few a minutes they lay there in the hall, unable to hear because of the ringing in their ears. From underneath the door they could see a light, and then they heard a blood curdling scream come from Sam. Mike's last thought before he passed out was "How can there be light? There's no electricity."

CHAPTER EIGHTEEN

om Dixon met his four fellow Guardsmen at the appointed time. He explained to them that what he was asking of them was top secret. "It's probably breaking all kinds of rules and regulations, but it won't be the first time the military has crossed the line," he smiled.

"I want you to prepare for a burial at sea. The deceased is not a veteran; he's a civilian." The men looked at each. "There will be no paper work; and you'll treat this matter like it never happened. You cannot speak of this mission to anyone. Not to your wives or friends. Is that clear?"

"Yes, sir", they answered in unison.

"The location where the body is must never be revealed. Once the mission is over, I want you to 'forget' where this location is. I want a small boat to carry seven civilians and possibly two dogs a mile out to the waiting ship. The ship will then sail the required thirteen miles out to sea. Now the men were really puzzled. Was the body somebody high up in office or what? Had to be someone important for sure.

"I'll take you to the location one hour from now. That'll give you time enough to round up your gear. There is no casket. The body is to be wrapped in a shroud. Oh, one more thing; be ready to climb a steep cliff. You'll need ropes to lower the body," said Tom. He could almost hear the men's brains buzzing with questions, but he knew his men. They would follow his orders to the letter without question. "Burial will be at 1100 hours tomorrow morning."

Tom drove the men as far as the black SUV could go before coming to the large rocks on the shore. They got out and walked to a sheer cliff which had an opening about 70 feet up. It was a fairly easy climb for them as they had done these kinds of maneuvers in boot camp and they were all still in good physical shape. Tom Dixon was older and wasn't as agile as his men, but still, he made the climb while the men waited just inside the cave opening. He led them to a secret door, and when it slid open and the men entered the inner cave they gasped in surprise to see an Indian village below them. Almost in shock, they walked down the stone steps to where the wigwams stood.

Tom led them to the tent where he and Fred had placed Chatunga just a couple of hours before. The Guardsmen gently wrapped the body in a heavy duty blue cloth which is called a shroud. There were metal loops on it for feeding straps through and criss-crossing them like shoe laces to tie it shut. The straps could hold flowers and messages if so desired.

Tom drove the men back to the Groton base, and then he continued on back home to tell the Pittengers and Adele about the completed plans and the time of burial. He was surprised Jimmy and Mike weren't home yet. He was hoping that the news of Chatunga had been told to them by now. "Fred, we better g o see if we can find them. They've been gone too long." Fred agreed and told the women they wouldn't be long.

"You might want to pick a lot of flowers while we're gone. Some will be on the shroud, and some put on top of the water," said Tom as he closed the door behind him.

CHAPTER NINETEEN

As Mike and Jimmy "slept" in the hallway, Sam was sitting in one of the wooden chairs on the other side of the door. It wasn't as if he had a choice to sit; he was forced there and he couldn't move. At first a bright light blinded him, but then he saw a figure walk from the middle of the light. A man's voice said, "Fear not."

"Wh . . . who are you?" stuttered a very frightened Sam. "What are you going to do to me?"

"My name is Archangel Zaphiel, Samuel; but you know me better as Fletcher."

"You're crazy. Fletcher is a kid. You're a guy in a dress." Sam was referring to Zaphiel's dark green robe that came down to his golden sandals. The angel stood over six feet tall. The only resemblance he now had to Fletcher was the beautiful red hair, and the blue eyes, which were now even bluer.

"I assure you that I am not crazy. Angels can take on many forms. I came this time as an eleven-year-old boy with a hump on his back. The hump was actually my folded wings which cannot be removed." With those words, Zaphiel spread out his wings; they were three feet long on each side. "Ahh, that feels good," he said as he flexed them up and down.

Sam thought to himself, 'Okay, this can't be happening. There must have been something bad in that last drug Eddie told me to try and now I'm having hallucinations.'

He called out to Jimmy and Mike for help.

"They can't hear you, Sam. The boys were put to sleep temporarily until our little session is over. I hope you're okay with the chair you're sitting in. I wanted it comfortable for you, but not too comfortable. I want you to be alert and pay attention to everything I'm going to tell and even show you." Zaphiel sat down in the other chair beside Sam.

"Let me begin with why I came to this town and this school. I'm the leader of a choir of angels called cherubims. We watch over children and will help them in any way we can. If they are having trouble in school with friends, at home, or even physical or emotional issues, we are there to watch over them and protect them. We've been watching you and how your bullying is starting to go down a very slippery slope that will end in disaster for you . . . and your family.

"I'm going to start by showing you some of the people you've hurt. You will actually feel their pain. It will be like you are them. Close your eyes." Sam had no choice; he couldn't keep his eyes open no matter how hard he tried.

The first vision was of him scaring Erin when she was only two-years-old by holding her underwater in their kiddy pool. He felt her fear, and her panic of not being able to breathe. Sam gulped for air. It was horrible. Then the scene changed to when he pushed Erin down the stairs. Again, he felt her panic and when the bone in her arm snapped, he felt like it was his own arm breaking. It hurt so badly.

Next, he became Diane Jenkins. Sam felt the pain in Diane's heart when he called her names. It was horrible.

Zaphiel even made him feel what the animals felt when they were tortured from the smallest to the biggest, especially Spunky. He felt the dog's pain when he was kicked, and the hurt of being rejected when all the dog wanted was to give him love.

He felt his mother's sadness and confusion about not knowing how to stop her son from being rude and mean. Sam began to cry and begged the angel to stop. He couldn't take it any more.

"I'm afraid there's more, Samuel. I now have to show you what will become of you if you continue to act as you do. You were planning to kill Mike and Jimmy tonight who have done you no harm. In fact, it was Jimmy's prayer in church one Sunday that alerted me that help was needed. He prayed for you, Sam. He prayed that you would stop the bullying and that your heart would be softened by God and you would change. So here is your future if you don't change:"

Sam saw himself getting into more drugs, really heavy duty ones that would control his life. He saw himself robbing people's homes to get money for the expensive habit. As he got older, he stole cars. He was speeding in a car he had stolen one night while he was 'high' and hit an elderly man who stood beside the road where he was waiting to cross. He never stopped to help. The man died. Sam was eventually caught and arrested. His sentence was twenty years behind bars. When he got out of prison, he couldn't get a job because of his record and he had no skills at anything. He became homeless, living on the streets. They found him dead from an over-dose. Alone . . . and scared.

Sam was now sobbing and said repeatedly, "I'm sorry. I'm so sorry."

Zaphiel wrapped his wings around Sam's shaking body. "You can open your eyes now, Samuel. I felt your sincere shame and regret. I think things will be a whole lot different in your future.

Sam's tear-filled eyes looked up at Zaphiel. "I promise you that I'm going to be a different kid. I want to go home and hug my parents and sister and tell them I am sorry for all the things I have put them through. I want to give Spunky the biggest hug he's ever had in his life."

"I'm glad you included your dad in the hugs. All those whippings he gave you made him feel really bad afterward. But, he didn't know any other way to stop your bad conduct. He was abused as a kid, and he thought that was the way bad kids were handled. You will be the one to teach him about love. You will see a change in him . . . a change for the better. I promise.

"You can start your new life at this very minute by going out there to tell Mike and Jimmy you are sorry. And don't forget to thank Jim for the prayers."

"I will, Flet . . . , I mean, Zaphiel."

"Before you leave, Samuel, I want to ask you if you know the meaning of your name."

Sam shook his head 'no'.

"It means 'God's heart, or 'God heard'. He heard you today, and I know He's smiling."

"I like that," smiled Sam. "Yep, I really do." He turned around before walking out of the room. "Thank you, Zaph . . . . for everything."

CHAPTER TWENTY

J im and Mike were awakened by a gentle touch from Zaphiel. When they saw the angel standing over them, they both thought Sam had killed them and now they were in Heaven. Zaphiel said 'fear not'. (Those two words are always spoken by an angel to a mortal). Sam was standing next to him, but he looked different some how . . . softer even. "Sam has something to say to you both; please accept his words as true."

"Jim, Mike, I am sorry for all the things I have said and done to you. I understand if you don't believe that, but over time I'm determined to prove I'm not the bully that I was. Like the old saying goes, 'today is the first day of the rest of my life.' Sam reached down and offered his hand to help them stand up.

Each boy accepted his hand of help. They didn't know what to say. As usual, Mike was the first one to find his voice. "Right now, I'm so confused about what has happened here, but Jim and I have witnessed some amazing things in the past, even supernatural stuff, so nothing surprises us anymore. But I have so many questions. I'm sure Jim has some, too."

"I can't tell you what took place between Sam and me because it is private. But I will explain a couple mysteries that you are entitled to know the answers to. Zaphiel started first about the hump on his back when he took on the personality of Fletcher.

"The reason there was no record of a Fletcher in school was because no one could see me except Sam, Ricky, Jason, and you two boys. That's why I couldn't play the Man From Mars game in gym or kickball. It would look pretty silly to the other kids if you threw the ball at someone who wasn't there.

"Yes, I stayed in the Killmer house, but angels don't have fingerprints. So there were none to find. It was Sam who made the call to the police. Like I said, I was visible to him and when he saw me go inside that house and knowing it had been vacant for many years, he wanted not only to get me into trouble, but also he could break in there later and I'd get the blame. I believe that's right, Sam?" Sam shook his head yes. Since you boys could see me at school, I had to carry a backpack like everyone else. I put the name Fletcher on some of the papers because I knew Sam would rifle through the bag looking for money. He had to believe that I was a real student.

"Now, you boys should go home. Your parents are waiting for you." Sam knew his parents weren't waiting for him and that made him sad. But he sure wanted to see them. "Sam, you can go ahead of Mike and Jimmy. There's something private I want to tell them."

"Okay. I'll wait outside for you guys and walk down through the woods with you." Before he turned to leave, he handed his knife to Zaphiel.

After Sam closed the front door, Zaphiel spoke. "Before your visit to Chatunga last week, I went to see him. This shocked the boys. His visit must have scared poor Chatunga. Zaphiel could read their minds. "Rest assured, Chatunga was not surprised to see me. Even though I was in the form of an eleven-year-old boy, he *knew* I was sent from God. When I told him it was time for him *to go home* soon, he was very happy. I promised I would escort him when the time came. So, James and Michael, always remember my words when you are sad about losing your friend.

The three boys walked down the hill, chattering like they'd been best friends forever. When they reached Jimmy's yard, Sam shook their hands and said, "See ya, Monday." Eileen saw them from the window, and couldn't believe her eyes. She knew all about Sam's bad reputation so it seemed very odd that the three boys were talking and smiling!

When the boys entered the kitchen Jimmy apologized for being away so long but that scary storm forced them to wait it out till it was over. Fred looked puzzled. "What storm?" Jimmy said, "Dad, how could you not know about a storm that big?" Then immediately the thought came into Jimmy's head, 'the storm was staged for just Mike and me to force us into the old house.'

"Well, I guess it was one of those freaky isolated storms," said Fred. "The sun was shining bright down here without a cloud in the sky. Anyway, please sit down. We have something to tell you." (Adele and Tom were still there at the table).

Fred told the boys about finding Chatunga. The adults were waiting for the boys to burst out crying upon hearing the news of Chatunga's death. When Jimmy said, "It's okay, Dad. Chatunga is fine." Fred thought at first Jim didn't understand what he had said, or he couldn't accept the fact that his friend was gone. "We know Chatunga is happy and at peace."

CHAPTER TWENTY-ONE

Commander Tom Dixon and Adele picked up the Pittenger family at 10:30 the next morning. Jimmy climbed in back with Laddie to sit next to Mike and Liberty. Caroline and Abigail sat in the middle seat with Fred and Eileen. It was very quiet in the SUV on the short ride to the shore. Even the dogs were subdued. A smaller boat was waiting to bring them to a bigger Coast Guard ship that was anchored about a half a mile out in the water. After the people came on board, the ship would travel another thirteen miles out to sea. Chatunga's body was already on board. Tom wanted to spare the families from seeing the men lower his body from the cave.

A Seaman helped the women, kids, and dogs board the big ship. Tom led them over to the shroud that contained Chatunga's body. It was lying on a stainless steel platform. The girls helped their mothers tuck some of the flowers they had brought with them into the straps of the shroud. The rest would later be tossed into the sea over Chatunga's watery grave. Mike and Jim each put a plastic sealed picture of themselves into the straps. The adults looked puzzled when they saw a yogurt label placed among the flowers.

Tom asked if anyone would like to say something. Mike was the first one to speak up. "I just want to say I'll miss you, Chatunga. You were the best buddy a guy could have. It felt good when you would always greet Jim and me with a big smile. I thank you for the food you gathered and shared with us. (It's always about food with Mike thought Jimmy). Mike was a little self-conscious of the others standing there so he ended abruptly, "well, I guess that's all I want to say."

Jimmy was the next one to speak. "I don't know how to tell you or thank you for sharing stories of long ago. For me, you were like a history book that came alive (It's always about books, thought Mike). I know your friend, Azumboa, is waiting for you so you can go hunting together again where you are safe from all harm. I'm not sure, though, if there's hunting allowed in Heaven. If it's not, you'll still have fun being kids again. We will never, ever forget you. If Laddie and Liberty could speak, I know they would tell you how much they loved going with me and Mike to visit you."

Some sobs could be heard coming from the adults. Fred said, "I think Jimmy and Mike said it all better than we can. Good-bye, dear friend."

"Amen," responded the adults.

Commander Dixon signaled for the ship's bell to ring eight times. Then the platform was tilted up and Chatunga's body gently slid feet first into the water. Tom tossed a few flowers overboard to mark the exact spot of the 'grave. Jimmy and Mike buried their faces into their dogs' fur and wept openly. Laddie and Liberty softly whimpered.

The engines that had been idling were now put into gear, and the props started turning. Slowly, the ship made a circle around the place where the flowers floated on the water.

As the ship circled, everyone grabbed handfuls of flowers and threw them where the first flowers had landed. Laddie and Liberty each had one of their favorite chew toys in their mouths. The boys helped the dogs to stand on their hind legs at the railing of the ship so they could drop the toys into the sea.

Because Chatunga wasn't a military man, a recording of Dvorak's music 'Going Home' was played over the loud speakers instead of 'Taps". Adele had printed out the lyrics to the song the night before and now gave everyone a copy of the words so they could sing along:

Going home, going home
I'm just going home.
Quiet-like, slip away
I'll be going home
It's not far, just close by
Jesus is the Door

Work all done, laid aside,
Fear and grief no more
Friends are there, waiting now
He is waiting, too
See His smile, see His hand
He will lead me through

Morning Star lights the way
Restless dream all done
Shadows gone, break of day
Life has just begun.

Every tear wiped away,
Pain and sickness gone
Wide awake there with Him

Peace goes on and on
Going home, going home
I'll be going home
See the Light, See the Sun
I'm just going home

Goin' home, goin' home
I'm just goin' home
Quiet like, some still day
I'm just goin' home

It's not far, just close by
Through an open door
Work all done, care laid by
Going to fear no more
Mother's there, expectin' me
Father's waitin' too
Lots of folk gathered there
All the friends I knew . . . .

AFTER WORD

Teachers and students alike couldn't believe the miraculous change in Sam Newman. Jennie never did get that note 'from Mike'. Sam had torn it up and threw it away. He still remained friends with Jason and Ricky, but now instead of bossing them around, he made them feel equal and a whole lot better as far as their confidence went.

Because he worked hard and studied, Sam was able to advance to middle school with his class. Jimmy had helped him work toward that goal.

Sam's parents were the most amazed at the change in their son. He removed all piercings, had his hair cut, and heavy metal was never heard again; he even took the garbage out without being asked. He became a good brother to Erin, and a kinder, gentler master to Spunky. Almost every day he took the dog for long walks, or played fetch with him in the backyard.

Before school started in the fall, his father took him to Fenway Park to watch the Red Sox play against the New York Yankees! Zaphiel was right about the promise; Sam wasn't the only one who had changed; his father did, too.

Jimmy kept and treasured Chatunga's Bible. The Indian had printed on the first page of the inside cover, 'My guide for walking on the Red Road'. The boys rarely went to the cave, and when they did, it felt cold and empty. It just wasn't the same without their old friend who always had a camp fire burning, and a story to tell. The visits became further and further apart until they stopped altogether. After that, the only time they went back to the cave was years later when they were men and lived far apart from each other. They would meet once a year in the cave on the date of Chatunga's death, light the campfire, and sit to talk about what was going on in their lives.

The cave that had been home to Chatunga for so many years was kept secret. Tom and Fred agreed that some day the town would have to be told about it and all the gold within its walls. But, that would be a long, long time in the future, if ever . . . .

PERSONAL NOTE

We have a special request to all you kids in or returning to school. If you see someone who is struggling to make friends or being bullied because he/she doesn't have many friends or because they are shy, or not as pretty, or not dressed in the most "in" clothes—PLEASE step up. Say "hi" or at least smile at them in the hallway. You never know what that person might be facing outside of school. Your kindness might just make a big difference in someone's life!

Thanks,
Jim, Mike, and Fletcher

ABOUT THE AUTHOR

D.C. Marek lives in Connecticut and is the author of a series
of stories about James Pittenger and Mike Decker.

Her goal is to inspire young readers to be the best they can be.

Other Books by D.C. Marek

Secrets of the Cave

Haunted Holiday, A Revolutionary Christmas

Four to the Rescue

Printed in the United States
By Bookmasters